Dog Walker, Inc.

by Christine M. Calson
illustrated by Laura Gibbons Nikiel

 HOUGHTON MIFFLIN BOSTON

Printed in China

ISBN-13: 978-0-547-02574-2
ISBN-10: 0-547-02574-2

13 14 15 16 0940 19 18 17 16
4500569761

When Connor Lee knocked on Mrs. Garcia's door, loud barking greeted him. Mrs. Garcia opened the door. She shoved three leashes at him. At the end of each leash was a tiny yipping dog.

"Three dogs?" Connor asked, surprised. He was expecting only one.

"I'm dogsitting my sister's Chihuahuas, too," Mrs. Garcia said. "This one is Lupe, that one is Ramón, and the little one is Chica."

Connor got them all mixed up as soon as she told him the names. He didn't have to know which was which, he decided. He just had to walk them.

Connor is surprised to see three Chihuahuas.

In his pocket, Connor had a stash of plastic bags to clean up after the dogs. He hoped he didn't have to use too many.

Connor walked down the hall. He would pick up two more dogs at Mr. Wong's apartment. He couldn't believe his good fortune. His flyer—*Dog Walker, Inc.*—had only been posted around the neighborhood for one day. The flyer offered a dog walk for $3. Connor did some mental math. Three dogs plus Mr. Wong's two dogs equaled five dogs. He would walk them five days a week, at three dollars per walk, per dog.

Connor figured he'd soon have enough money to pay the adoption fee for a dog of his own.

3 dogs + 2 dogs = 5 dogs

5 dogs x 5 walks = 25 walks

25 walks x 3 dollars = 75 dollars

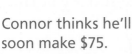

Connor thinks he'll soon make $75.

Connor could already imagine life with his own dog. Together, they would play catch in the park. He would scratch the dog behind its soft ears. Connor planned to let the dog up on the bed when his mom wasn't paying attention. And he would make sure to drop scraps under the kitchen table. He even

Connor daydreams about owning a dog.

had a name picked out already—Striker, like one of the heroes in his favorite movie.

His mom was the one who had given him the job idea. *Show me you're responsible*, she had said. *Earn the money, and we'll talk about a pet.* So Connor had decided to walk dogs, and today was the first day of business.

It seemed like the perfect way to prove he was responsible. Plus, he could make money at the same time.

At Mr. Wong's apartment, two basset hounds, Samo and Suzie, waddled over to say hello. Their ears dragged across the floor.

Mr. Wong was all smiles. "Take them for a nice long walk," he urged Connor. "I can't walk them often enough anymore. Not since I developed arthritis." He handed Connor the leashes. In the hallway, the little dogs growled. Mr. Wong said with a smile, "Have fun. Be good dogs."

"Come on, everyone," Connor called. He kept three leashes in one hand and two in the other. He tried to lead all five dogs down the hall. Their paws slipped and skidded across the shiny tile floor as they all tried to keep up.

Samo and Suzie are ready for their walk.

Connor and the dogs headed toward the building's front door. A young woman with dark glasses was just coming in.

"Are you the dog walker?" she asked. "The one who put up the flyers?"

"That's me," Connor answered proudly. Samo sniffed the woman's foot. Suzie sniffed her purse. They could smell the woman's dog.

"I was hoping to see you. My roommate and I need our dog walked this week. Do you think you could take him, too?"

Six dogs at once? Could he hold that many leashes? Still, the more dogs he walked, the faster he would make money. Maybe he would set a new record for dog walking.

Connor agreed to walk the woman's dog. They went to her apartment to get the dog and the leash.

"Gussie can be a little rowdy sometimes," she warned. "But he's really incredibly sweet and gentle, for a St. Bernard."

Out on the sidewalk, the six dogs pulled their leashes in six different directions. Connor could barely hang on.

"Sit," he ordered. Suzie sat down on Connor's foot. None of the other dogs sat. The Chihuahuas yipped. Gussie, the St. Bernard, started drooling on Samo's back.

Maybe if he started walking, they would all calm down. He would take them to the park. Dogs liked parks.

"Heel," Connor said. He started walking. One of the Chihuahuas ran behind him and wrapped its leash around his legs. Suzie tripped on one of her ears. Gussie walked right into Suzie and got all twisted up in the leashes.

Connor gets tangled up in dog leashes.

Connor glanced around to see if anyone was watching. One lady walked by with a smile on her face.

"Having a little trouble there, son?" another man called from his bicycle.

Connor blushed and straightened out the leashes.

"I can do this," he muttered under his breath. "How hard can it be to walk a bunch of dogs?"

By the time they reached the park, Connor and the dogs had already stopped six times. They had to stop once to clean up after Samo. They had to stop again to keep Gussie from eating a banana peel. And they had to stop again and again to untangle the Chihuahuas, who kept running back and forth under Gussie's belly.

Gussie tries to snack on a banana peel.

The park was peaceful and quiet. A few kids played on the jungle gym. Several moms sat on benches. Some teenagers fed ducks in the pond. On the field, Connor could see a team practicing soccer.

The dogs also saw the kids playing soccer. They yanked hard on their leashes.

"Stop it," Connor scolded. "We're walking. You can't play."

Gussie tugged at his leash and bumped into one of the Chihuahuas. The little dog squealed. Within minutes, all six dogs were howling or barking or whining or yipping or crying.

The dogs want to play in the park.

"Shhh!" Connor begged. The women on the benches frowned at him. "Sit! Lie down! Stay!" But none of the dogs obeyed. Connor tried to pet the dogs to calm them. They circled him, each one wanting attention. The Chihuahuas tangled their leashes together again. Were dogs even allowed at this park? Connor couldn't remember.

A little girl ran up to them. "Can I pet your big doggie?"

"No, I'm not sure how friendly—" Connor began, but the girl had already wrapped her little arms around Gussie.

"He's so cute." Gussie was sniffing the girl's ponytail. "Can I play with him?"

"No. I'm working," Connor tried to explain. But just then, a soccer ball flew past Gussie. With a big yank of the leash, Gussie pulled free and ran after it.

Gussie chases a soccer ball.

With leashes wrapped around his legs,
Connor stumbles and falls.

"Chase, doggie! Chase!" the little girl called.
She took off running. Gussie was already on the
soccer field.

"Wait!" Connor shouted. "Stop!"

The five other dogs grew frantic. The leashes
around Connor's legs wrapped tighter and tighter.
He tried to run after Gussie but stumbled and fell.
Connor hit the ground hard. He lay still, dizzy.
The leashes yanked out of his hand.

Connor crawled to his knees and tried not to
panic. He felt like he was living through an episode
of a bad comedy show. One of the Chihuahuas was
playing tug-of-war with Connor's pants. Another
was chasing a squirrel. Samo returned, panting,
after chasing the ducks at the pond. Suzie was in
the sandbox eating crackers out of a toddler's hand.

11

Gussie thinks the soccer team wants to play with him.

In the distance, Connor could see Gussie with a soccer ball in his mouth. The little girl and the whole soccer team ran after him.

Where was the other Chihuahua? Connor squinted at the field. It was nowhere in sight. Suddenly, Connor saw a teenager's backpack jerk along the ground. It started turning, and a tiny yellow Chihuahua came into view.

"*Don't* fetch, Chica-or-Lupe-or-Ramón!" Connor yelled, wishing he had learned which dog was which.

"Do you need some help?" One of the moms had gotten up from her bench. She helped Connor to his feet.

"Yeah." He hated to admit it, but things had gotten out of hand. "Thanks."

"Are all these dogs yours?"
the woman asked.

"No. I'm a dog walker."

"It seems like they're walking
you," she laughed.

The woman had a box of cheese crackers in her
bag. Using the crackers as treats, she and Connor
coaxed the dogs back. By the time they had caught
the six dogs, all the crackers were gone.

*   *   *   *   *

Connor returned the dogs to their owners.

"Was my Gussie a good doggie?" cooed the
woman in the dark glasses. "Did he get a nice
long walk?"

"Yep," replied Connor, "he got a very, very
long walk."

When Connor finally got home, he plopped
down beside his mom at the kitchen table.

She thumbed through a magazine and glanced
up at him. "How's the job?"

"I blew it, Mom."

"Why?"

"I almost lost all the dogs. It was crazy. They were going everywhere." He sighed. "I could have handled one or two dogs—maybe. But not six. I had to ask someone for help."

Connor's mom smiled. "That sounds very responsible."

He wrinkled his forehead. "What do you mean? I messed up."

She nodded. "But you understand that you took on too much. And you're willing to admit making a mistake."

He sat up straight, hope leaping in his chest. "Does that mean I can still get a pet?"

His mother laughed. "What kind of dog were you thinking of?"

Connor tipped his head and grinned. "Actually, I think I might prefer a cat."

Connor decides that cats are easier to take care of!

Responding

✔ **TARGET SKILL** **Author's Purpose** The author, Christine M. Calson, wanted to entertain readers with a funny story. Copy the chart below. Then add details that support her purpose.

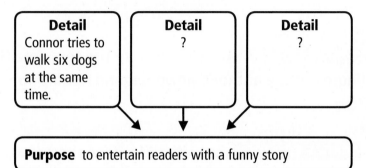

Detail	**Detail**	**Detail**
Connor tries to walk six dogs at the same time.	?	?

Purpose to entertain readers with a funny story

✎ **Write About It**

Text to Self Think of a plan to earn money for something you want to buy. Write a letter to a friend describing your plan.

assuming	launch
developed	mental
episodes	record
feature	thumbed
incredibly	villains

✓ **TARGET SKILL** **Author's Purpose** Use text details to figure out the author's viewpoint and reasons for writing.

✓ **TARGET STRATEGY** **Monitor/Clarify** As you read, notice what isn't making sense. Find ways to figure out the parts that are confusing.

GENRE **Realistic Fiction** is a present-day story with events that could take place in real life.